Himalayan Tales

Collected, edited & translated by Rashid Naeem

Sparrow

Illustrated by Alan Greenwell

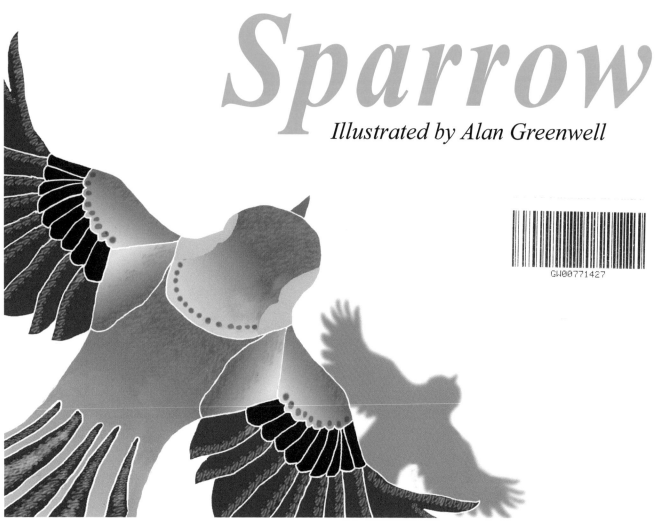

In Gilgit-Baltistan, 'sparrow' means a small bird (harachan in the Shina language).

Himalayan Tales
Collected, edited & translated by Rashid Naeem

Rashid comes from Gilgit-Baltistan, a spectacular region within the Himalayas, the Hindu Kush and the Pamir mountains. The Karakoram Highway and the giant K2 mountain are nearby.

Rashid now lives in the UK. As a child, his parents told him many exciting and uplifting stories. These stories have been passed down from parent to child over generations without being written down.

Rashid has collected these stories and translated them from Shina (the Gilgit-Baltistan language). Initially there are ten stories and there are more to come. He has been helped greatly by his parents and by various other relatives in Gilgit-Baltistan.

These stories for children are magical, with talking birds and animals. They introduce drama and conflict; this is resolved and leads to a happy and contented life. Some stories get a little scary. All carry an uplifting theme of how we must care for others, especially those who are downtrodden by life.

One day, Sparrow was sitting on the wall.

She was dreaming of helping coming generations.

She had a walnut in her little hand.

By accident she dropped the walnut in a fire.

She said to the fire, 'Hello Mr Fire. Can you please return my walnut?'

Mr Fire said, 'Sorry, I cannot because I am just starting to be hot.'

Sparrow said, 'If you cannot return my walnut, I will splash water on you.'

Mr Fire said, 'Go ahead. See if I care.'

Sparrow turned to the water and said,
'Hi Mr Water, can you help me bring my
walnut from the fire?'

Mr Water said, 'I have no time and I have
only a few drops left.'

Sparrow said, 'If you will not help, I can
bring that goat and she will drink you up.'

Sparrow flew over to the goat and said,
  'Hi Miss Goat. Can you please drink that
  water for me?'

Miss Goat said, 'I am too busy eating grass.'

Sparrow said, 'Miss Goat, I can bring
  Mr Butcher to you. He can take you into
  his shop and sell you for food.'

But Miss Goat just continued eating the grass.

Sparrow flew over to Mr Butcher and said, 'Mr Butcher, will you please take that goat?'

Mr Butcher said, 'Sorry, I am too busy cutting up some beef and I have no time.'

Sparrow said, 'Very well, I will ask that cat to eat your beef.'

Sparrow was without fear and flew over to the cat.

Sparrow said, 'Hi Miss Mew Cat, can you eat that beef for me please?'

Miss Mew Cat said, 'No, I am too busy drinking milk.'

Sparrow said, 'Right. I am going to bring some children and they will chase you.'

Sparrow flew over to the children playing football.

She said, 'Hello sweet kids. Can you please chase this cat for me?'

The kids said, 'No, we are too busy.'

Sparrow said, 'OK. I will complain to your mothers.'

The kids said, 'We don't care.'

Sparrow flew to the mothers who were working in the field.

Sparrow said, 'Mothers, your children will not help me. Will you please tell them off?'

The women said, 'No. We are busy working on our crops.'

Sparrow said, 'Right, I will ask the wind to help me. She might damage your crops.'

The women said, 'We don't care. Go ahead.'

Sparrow flew up high into the wind.
She said, 'Hello Windy. I am very upset.
Today I find that we are not kind to each
other and we don't help each other enough.
We all share this world and we ought to
help each other.'

Windy said, 'Don't be upset. This is life.
Sometimes we are good and sometimes we
are bad. Tell me, how can I help you?'

Sparrow said, 'I dropped my walnut into
the fire. I asked for help and no one would
help me get my walnut back.'

Windy said, 'You wait here. I will be back
soon. I will get your walnut back for you.'

Windy began to build up strength.

She started to blow the crops, first gently
  then with great bursts.

When the mothers saw their crops bending down, they understood why.

The mothers went to the children and told them off.

The kids understood why and they chased the cat.

The cat understood why.

She ran to the butcher's shop.

She started chewing the beef.

The butcher understood why and he grabbed
the goat.

The goat understood why.

She struggled free and she quickly started drinking the water.

The water understood why and quickly splashed the fire.

The fire understood why.

She returned the walnut to Sparrow.

Sparrow planted the walnut, then waited...

Sparrow now has lots of walnut trees.

People eat and take shade beneath them.

Sparrow has made a nest on top of the walnut tree and sings this song:

We must love each other
We must make peace in this world.